Roo
The Roaring Dinosaur

For Iso, and for Bombadil - DB

For Roberto & Eliza x - MS

SIMON AND SCHUSTER

First published in Great Britain in 2015 by Simon and Schuster UK Ltd

1st Floor, 222 Gray's Inn Road, London WC1X 8HB

A CBS Company

Text copyright © 2015 David Bedford

Illustrations copyright © 2015 Mandy Stanley

The right of David Bedford and Mandy Stanley to be identified as the author and illustrator of
this work has been asserted by them in accordance with the Copyright, Designs and Patents Act, 1988

A CIP catalogue record for this book is available from the British Library upon request

ISBN: 978-1-4711-1942-2 (HB)
ISBN: 978-1-4711-1943-9 (PB)
ISBN: 978-1-4711-1944-6 (eBook)
Printed in Italy
2 4 6 8 10 9 7 5 3

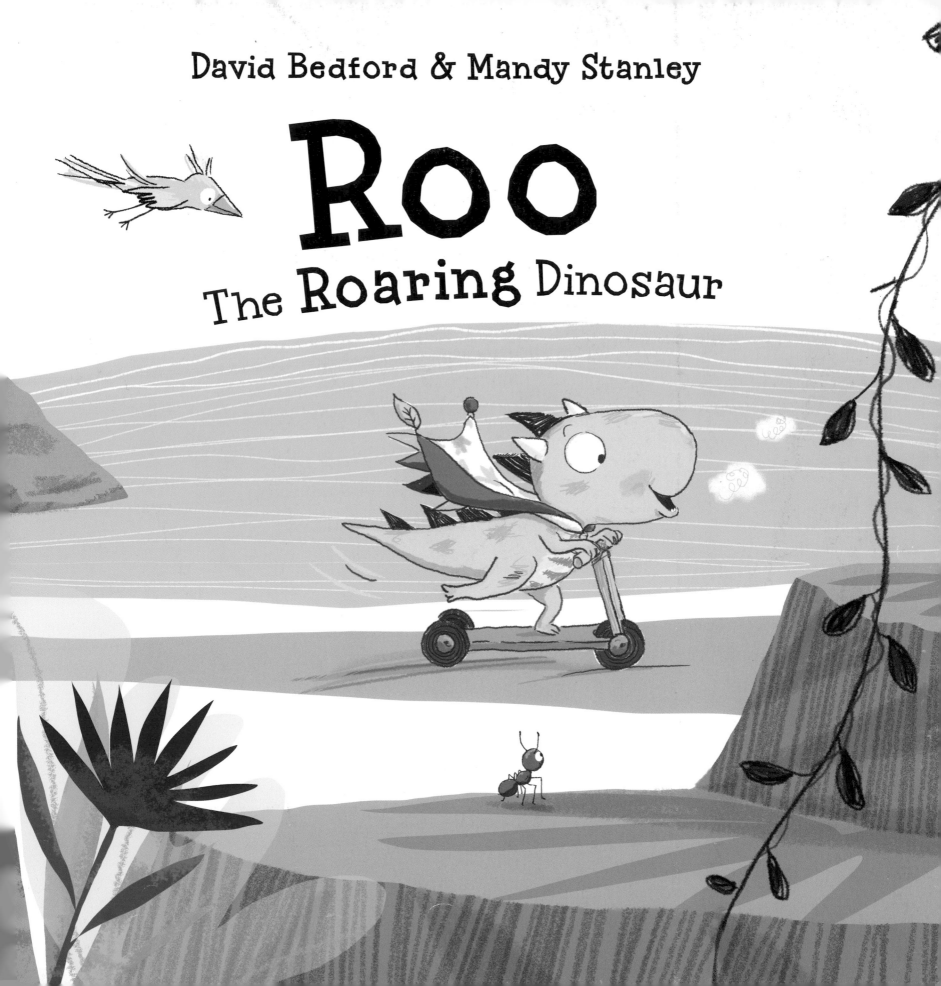

David Bedford & Mandy Stanley

Roo
The Roaring Dinosaur

Roo the Roaring Dinosaur loved his Moomie.
It was Roo's **favourite** thing ever.

Roo and his Moomie always
hid from the rain together . . .

and played in the sun together.

Roo never went anywhere
without his Moomie.

And wherever his Moomie went,
Roo always followed.

Then one day –

SWOOSH!
HISSSS!

It was a flying thing!
Red and blue and big and round.
And it was coming Roo's way!

'Roo run!' said Roo. 'Roo hide!'

Boing,

boing,

A new creature landed - BUMP -
right in front of Roo's nose.

'Oof!'

The new creature looked worried. 'My balloon is broken,' he said. He looked so sad that Roo decided to do something funny to cheer him up.

'Play Roo?' he said.

The creature tried a smile. 'All right Roo,' he said. 'I'm Wooly by the way.'

So Roo showed Wooly a
game to play in the sun . . .

and what to do when
the rain came down.

Then Roo took Wooly to . . .

his favourite place.

They sipped tasty coconut coolers.

And had lumpy, bumpy piggy-back rides.

Wooly showed Roo how
to make a camp.

They had supper on sticks
and sang fireside songs.

And when it got dark
they lay on the grass
and watched shooting stars
until they fell asleep.

The next morning Wooly looked sad again. 'I wish
I could stay and play but I really do have to go
home now,' he said. 'The trouble is, my balloon has
a hole in it. And I don't know how to fix it.'

Roo wanted to help. But there was only one thing
that was the right shape and size
to patch up the hole - and it was Roo's!

'Moomie mine!' said Roo. 'No give Moomie.'

Then Roo thought very hard. Moomie belonged to Roo.
But now Wooly needed it more.

So Roo made a very big decision. He hugged his
Moomie one last time. Then 'Give Moomie,' he said.

'Thank you, Roo,' said Wooly. 'You're the best friend ever.'

And together they stitched Moomie over the hole
in Wooly's balloon.

But the balloon still wouldn't fly.

I forgot!' said Wooly. 'It needs lots and lots of hot air.'

And that's when Roo had a brilliant idea.

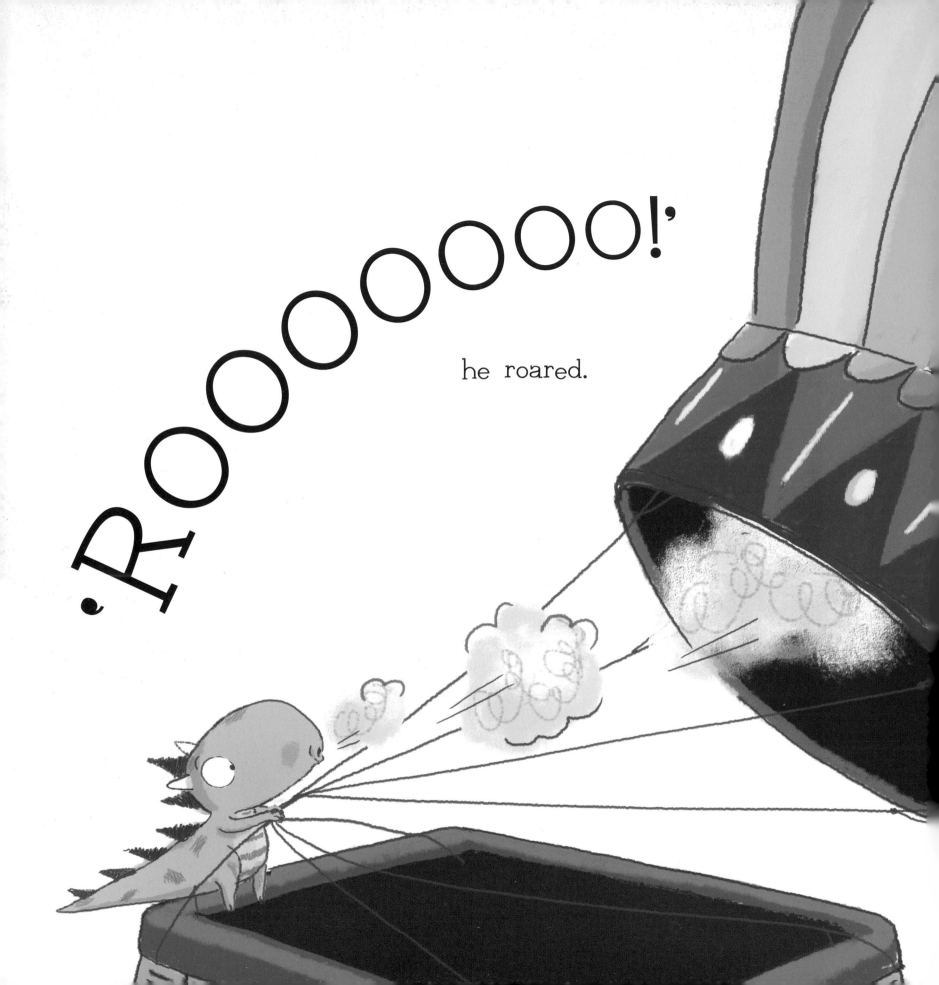

'ROOOOOOOO!'

he roared.

Suddenly the balloon
rose up in the air,
'Now I know why
you're called Roo!'
Wooly laughed.

'Bye, Roo!' he called. 'I won't forget you!'

'Bye!' Roo called back. 'Roo miss you.'

And then, more quietly. 'Bye, Moomie,' he said.

Wooly and the balloon were soon
far, far away.

So was Roo's Moomie.

Then suddenly Roo looked up and saw something floating down towards him.

This is for you ROO
Love Wooly x

'New Moomie!' roared Roo, happily.

'Roo love new Moomie!'

And off he went to play with his new favourite thing ever.

The End